The Abyssal Recitations

Concrete Mist Press
Heath Brougher
York, PA 17403
USA

Abyssal Recitations © 2024 Heller Levinson

All rights reserved. No part of this book may be reproduced or transmitted in any form or by any means, electronic or mechanical, without written permission from the author, except for the inclusion of brief quotations in a review.

Cover design and layout: Heath Brougher & harry k stammer

ISBN #: 979-8-218-33006-4

First edition

The Abyssal Recitations

Heller Levinson

Concrete Mist Press
2024

"It is the nature of the finite to have within its essence the seeds of extinction; the hour of its birth is the hour of its death."—Hegel

"Nothing exists except atoms and empty space; everything else is opinion."—Democritus

"Nothing is more real than nothing."—Samuel Becket

Abyssal Cavort

leapfrog lung chastity **GO**

for broke

giddy up ginger pop farfalle

trellis leer spread the

xylophones   brimstone rhubarb rhinestone

honky-tonk saxophone wily mesmerize with

interior plush

with cataleptic overleaf

with practiced irreverence

jump daily

madly

harmfully

hold back the tears

jump like frog

like groundswell

like vagabond

like demigods   wildebeests   holy rollers

jiminy cricket the cat dragged in

up in the sky

Way There

all along

delirial

mad about Madagascar

pouncing furiously

remembrances strung far back

Abyssal Rumpus

leapfrog lungchastity **GO**

for broke

giddyup farfalle trellis leer spread

xylophone cheer buckwheat bamboozle

bluster-

full breeze pony-Up

saxophone wily shear catalepsy drily play

a tune court a

rune swallow a swoon

m e s m e r i z e →

with interior plush

with adamancy

with efflorescent irreverence

jump gaily

jump daily

jump jump jigger jujube jalopy gale

flush mad

mad

mad

Abyssal Flare

fiery flint foam bucket ignition capsule

irridesce tensility abrupt glint corrupts

dark privilege

loin dark

obliquitous

fleck frolic whisk *kumbaya*

invigoration in

the

hollows of

oblivion

how much of

the abyss

is

voidable

can the

voidable

be

a-*voided*

Abyss:

the annulment that instigates;

the absence that fulfills

ABYSSALLEAK abort

triggered fleckspray. ring

rungcleared rusthinge clatter through chain,

the sprungclue, the

sprintdriven.

Arousal-spelunking clave

claw before the fleers.

Abyssal Leak

lesion   lambent ebb

deflationary rib folly

eke-let

Abyssal Recitation

footprint

pitching liquid vernacular

rounding vascular pith

-- a layman's circumference

capitulation severance

a tear endemic as currency

Abyssal Encounter

rash abject filtration sieve

speck disseminate

mud

off-center dribbledowns juggler decimate

vacancy brash preposterous

wish you were here

count of three

vast choruses dilute dissolve flight-furtive

fade-a-way fugitive cliffs

plea fog

Abyssal Sway

lopward metric-loose

zephyr

measure unsavoring

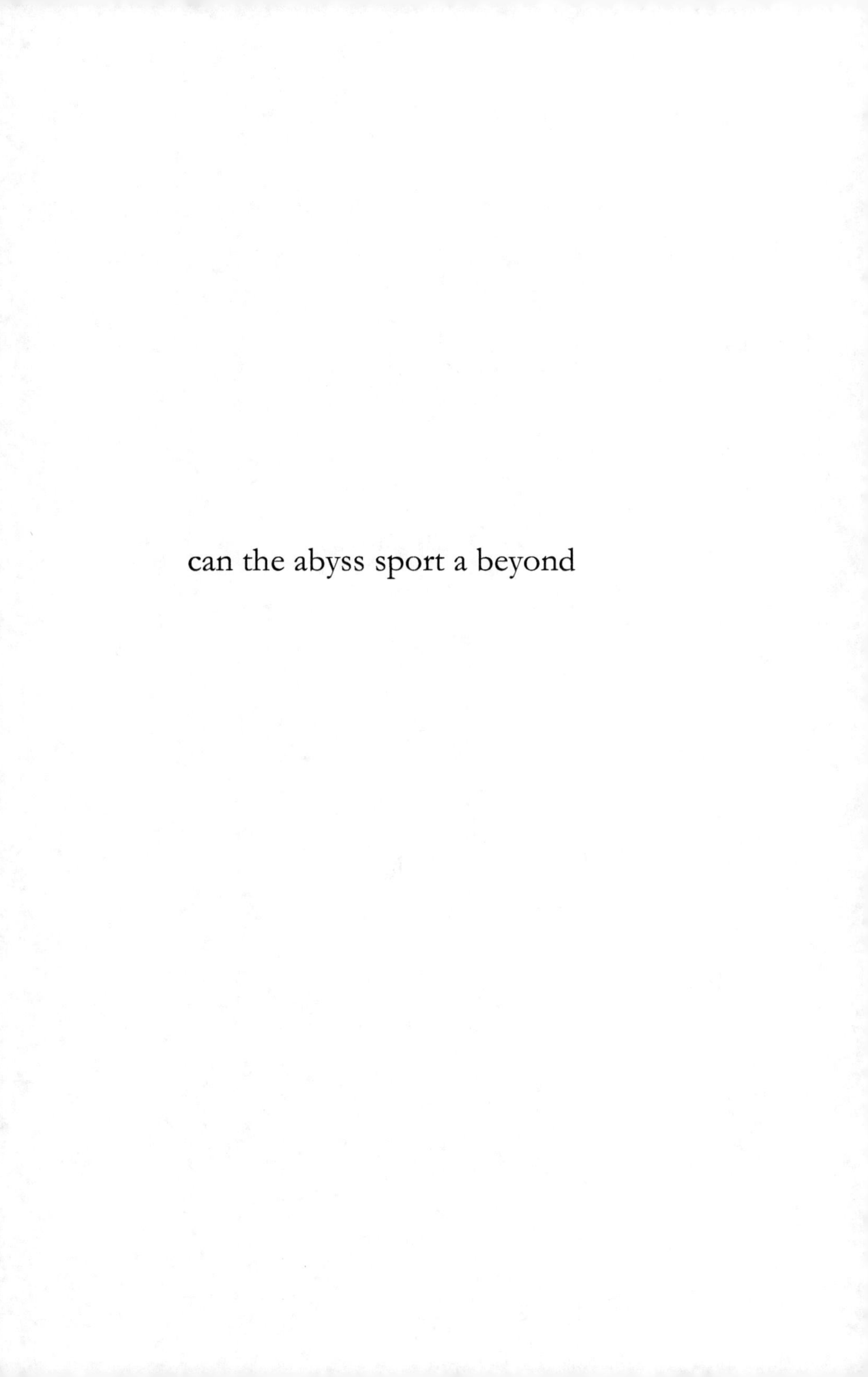

can the abyss sport a beyond

how much of

the abyss

is

loft

where in the

abyss

is

aeration

Abyssal Cavort

frothway freeze-dried cauterize crimp

cataract loose change

pubic meander public slander

crest dividend spiral spin

chance

prance

enhance

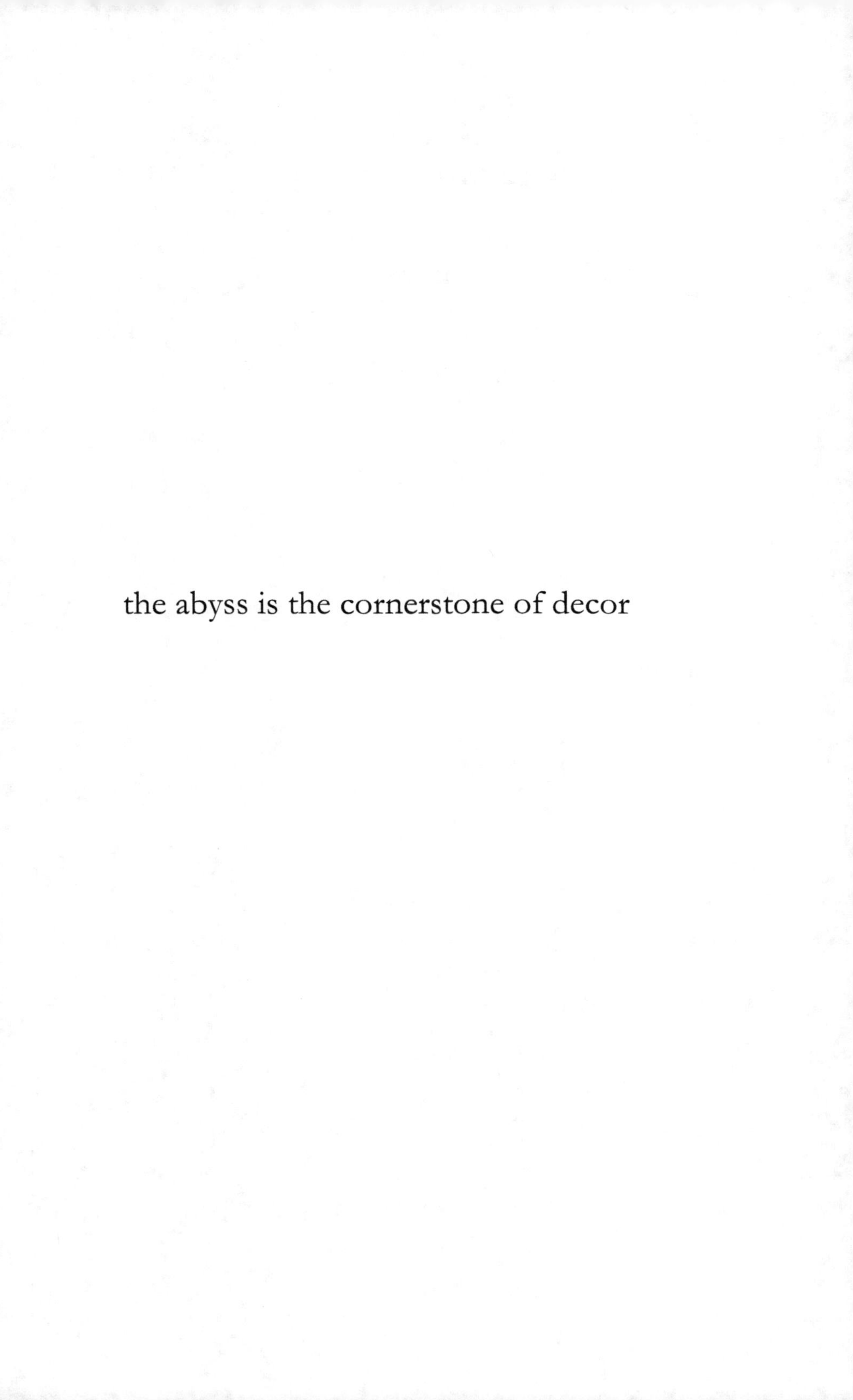

the abyss is the cornerstone of decor

Abyssal Reminiscence

shortfall evanescent repeal

reel pitch flinch

grate grill cultivate

sow sew stitch

foamcoalesce

surface

Abyssal Court

luckless the emblem sanctifies split-

second lustre

the backdraft steady

convinced

of its intention

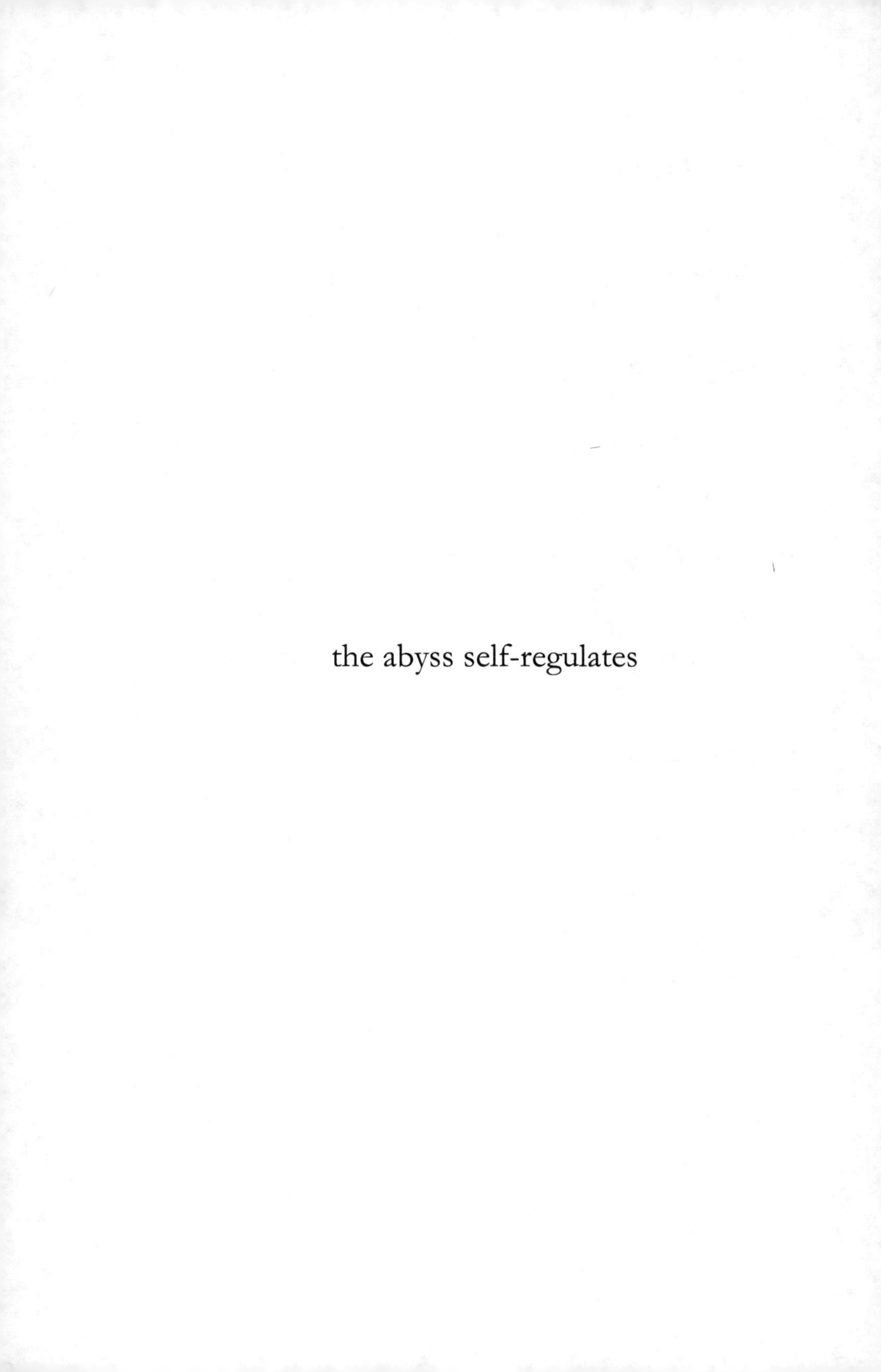

the abyss self-regulates

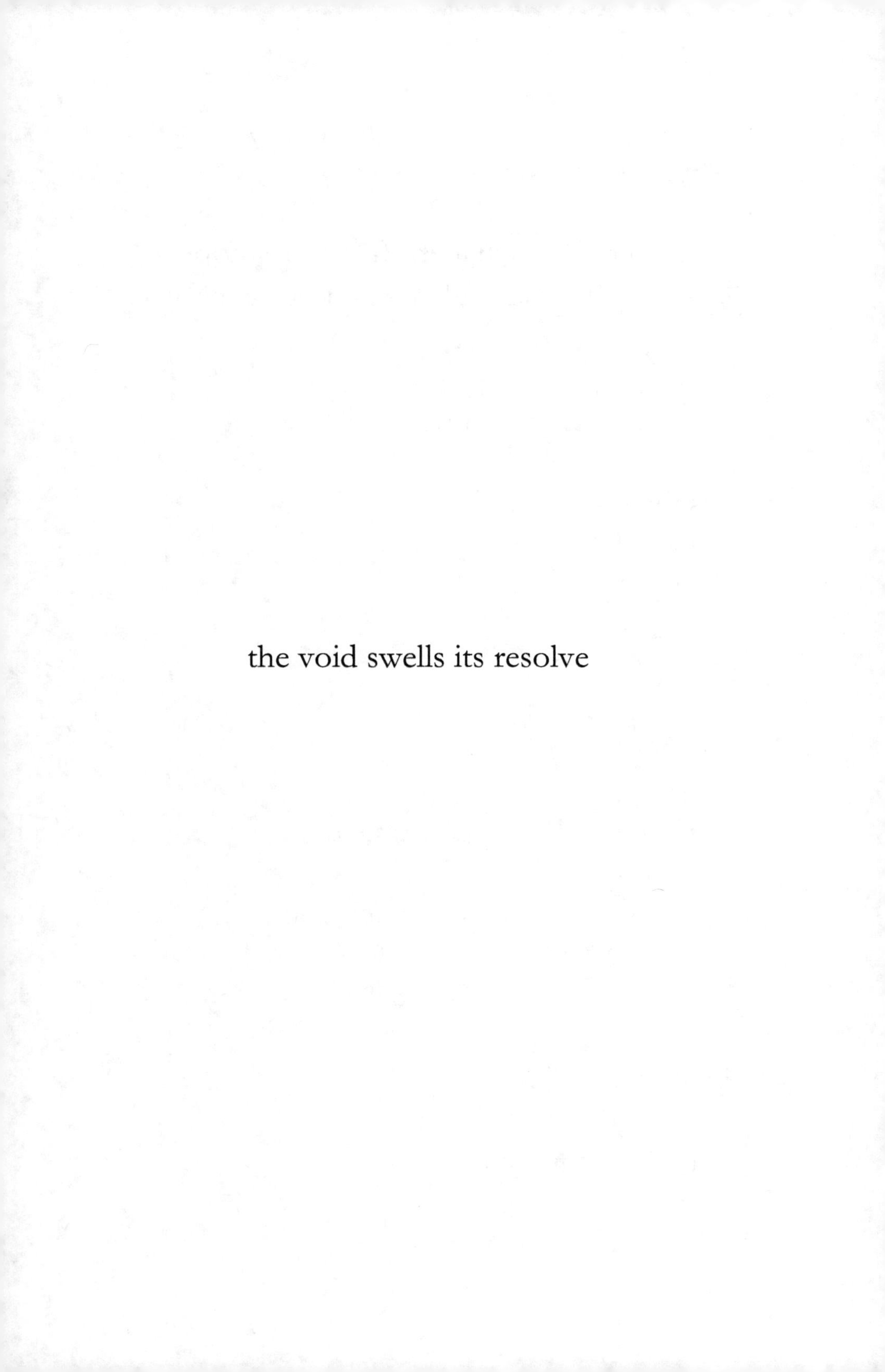

the void swells its resolve

Abyssal Asylum

miter undercut subaltern fracture isotope
strew landbound leaden gratuitous consensus
cults grow que-

asy querulous pock

suspicious

weigh

weighted

eerily down drawn

duct tape

fallow

inner hydraulics

lethargy magnified

reduced to

infinitesimal subtraction

to

self-abnegating

calculi

does the abyss recess

Abyssal Reduction

taper

trimdown

tuck

spleen evaporate

prune

Abyssal Subtraction

minus   less than

the erode that abrogates

the mark be-

comes

omission

how much of

the abyss

is

unaccounted for

nothing is full of nothing

nothing is knotted to not

Abyssal Abject

scour   sulk-sour

sunk

odiferous

rune registrant succumb

ambrosial waft

denude

abate spoor

spiral weightless concupiscence leaf filing

frond hurtle weir-whet whey fold, . . .

penitence, go lightly,   hatched recollections

lace lacerate

verbs incinerate incline grief vowels wish you

were here twine thickens straits thru mewling

chaw wipe bibelot courtesies in the company

of balance thistle thrush threshold thicket

cymbal clunk cadaver slaver skins thins

remote reflex, . . . exits no longer plush but

ceremonial, . . . template

reasserts: the challenge of sorts

          o f   b a r b a r o u s   c l a r i t y

pharyngealglobetilt globule melt

meat hooks

plenish pell-mell skirt failed fructose nugatory
signage stumped migratory . . . signatories
under investigation dirge doldrums drill
designate runner-ups run a fever few & far
between the company of percussion drum-
stalks hear from the hills thrill thrall thrum the
drum lowly pleasures of pace keep the peace,
holy consults hollow, to cherish is to labile, . .
run afoot,

from swallow vast vacuum

suck declivitous this

→

dearth dungeon

Abyssal Thanatos

dank dark drive mangle

truncheon spate

abrade

breach

temorous outreach

splinter

defer

deform

dematriculate

relent

to a

vacuumed proficiency

how much of

the abyss

is

caterwaul

Abyssal Pierce

lance visceral

outlier dengue

axial wobble torpor flange

(eddy skirl

lateralizing approximate emptiness blurs

blink simoom

in the sheer shimmer hush rim

motile sluice, . . . **Abyssal**

Rouse ,   stir curry

                                  clench claw

jam phantasm feint

indiscretion cull

grunt paw

the physics of export   (saddles of skin

                                  (stirrups of tears

diurnal twist

dislodge

Brood Asylum

ponderous rum pugnacity drill

deliberate   thick

glum cordon

web lactose

smear accumulate

braiding density loops   swoop

    swivel   roil lugubrious

lowly slung

Abyssal Dislodge run

amok reel totter rip-

tide

prick careen

cartwheel bob feather plaster

Abyssal Wrath

painstaker   thunder crack cyclops bellow

            peal blast tonitruous volley

rumble heap piles quake early dismissals

beatbacks

pulverizings

clownings you couldn't forestall

from battering cannonade

cardinal collide

this

precipitous discharge

lessness: the not nothing that is not much

abyss is not

absence

but the

plenitude

of

absence

Abyssal Stalk

trussed in manhandle

avoiding the silk of the day

the omissions were nasty & untoward

they had a way of masking oblivion

as if they could appear

whenever you called

www.ingramcontent.com/pod-product-compliance
Lightning Source LLC
LaVergne TN
LVHW010123170826
845678LV00012B/2559

* 9 7 9 8 2 1 8 3 3 0 0 6 4 *